'People should
 not leave looking-
glasses hanging in
their rooms any more
than they should
leave open cheque
books or letters
confessing some
 hideous crime'

VIRGINIA WOOLF
Born 25 January 1882, London
Died 28 March 1941, near Lewes, East Sussex

'The Lady in the Looking-Glass: A Reflection' first
published in *Harper's Magazine* in 1929, and reprinted
posthumously in *A Haunted House and Other Short Stories*
(1944). 'A Society' first published in *Monday or Tuesday* (1921).
'The Mark on the Wall' first published in *Two Stories* in 1917,
with woodcuts by Dora Carrington. 'Solid Objects' first
published in the *Athenaeum* in 1920, and later reprinted
in *A Haunted House and Other Short Stories*. 'Lappin and
Lapinova' first published in *Harper's Bazaar* in 1939, and later
reprinted in *A Haunted House and Other Short Stories*.

ALSO PUBLISHED BY PENGUIN BOOKS
*The Voyage Out · Night and Day · Jacob's Room · Mrs Dalloway ·
To the Lighthouse · Orlando · The Waves · The Years · Between
the Acts · Selected Short Stories · A Room of One's Own/Three
Guineas*

VIRGINIA WOOLF

The Lady in
the Looking-Glass

A Reflection

PENGUIN BOOKS

PENGUIN CLASSICS

Published by the Penguin Group
Penguin Books Ltd, 80 Strand, London WC2R ORL, England
Penguin Group (USA) Inc., 375 Hudson Street, New York, New York 10014, USA
Penguin Group (Canada), 90 Eglinton Avenue East, Suite 700, Toronto, Ontario,
Canada M4P 2Y3 (a division of Pearson Penguin Canada Inc.)
Penguin Ireland, 25 St Stephen's Green, Dublin 2, Ireland (a division of Penguin Books Ltd)
Penguin Group (Australia), 250 Camberwell Road, Camberwell, Victoria 3124, Australia
(a division of Pearson Australia Group Pty Ltd)
Penguin Books India Pvt Ltd, 11 Community Centre, Panchsheel Park,
New Delhi – 110 017, India
Penguin Group (NZ), 67 Apollo Drive, Rosedale, North Shore 0632, New Zealand
(a division of Pearson New Zealand Ltd)
Penguin Books (South Africa) (Pty) Ltd, 24 Sturdee Avenue, Rosebank, Johannesburg 2196,
South Africa
Penguin Books Ltd, Registered Offices: 80 Strand, London WC2R ORL, England

www.penguin.com

Selected from *Selected Short Stories*, first published by Penguin Books 1993
This edition published in Penguin Classics 2011
007

All rights reserved

Typeset by Jouve (UK), Milton Keynes
Printed in England by Clays Ltd, St Ives plc

ISBN: 978-0-141-19629-9

www.greenpenguin.co.uk

MIX
Paper from
responsible sources
FSC
www.fsc.org
FSC™ C018179

Penguin Books is committed to a sustainable
future for our business, our readers and our planet.
This book is made from Forest Stewardship
Council™ certified paper.

Contents

The Lady in the Looking-Glass: A Reflection   1

A Society   11

The Mark on the Wall   35

Solid Objects   49

Lappin and Lapinova   61

The Lady in the Looking-Glass: A Reflection

People should not leave looking-glasses hanging in their rooms any more than they should leave open cheque books or letters confessing some hideous crime. One could not help looking, that summer afternoon, in the long glass that hung outside in the hall. Chance had so arranged it. From the depths of the sofa in the drawing-room one could see reflected in the Italian glass not only the marble-topped table opposite, but a stretch of the garden beyond. One could see a long grass path leading between banks of tall flowers until, slicing off an angle, the gold rim cut it off.

The house was empty, and one felt, since one was the only person in the drawing-room, like one of those naturalists who, covered with grass and leaves, lie watching the shyest animals – badgers, otters, kingfishers – moving about freely, themselves unseen.

The room that afternoon was full of such shy creatures, lights and shadows, curtains blowing, petals falling – things that never happen, so it seems, if someone is looking. The quiet old country room with its rugs and stone chimney pieces, its sunken book-cases and red and gold lacquer cabinets, was full of such nocturnal creatures. They came pirouetting across the floor, stepping delicately with high-lifted feet and spread tails and pecking allusive beaks as if they had been cranes or flocks of elegant flamingoes whose pink was faded, or peacocks whose trains were veined with silver. And there were obscure flushes and darkenings too, as if a cuttlefish had suddenly suffused the air with purple; and the room had its passions and rages and envies and sorrows coming over it and clouding it, like a human being. Nothing stayed the same for two seconds together.

But, outside, the looking-glass reflected the hall table, the sunflowers, the garden path so accurately and so fixedly that they seemed held there in their reality unescapably. It was a strange contrast – all changing here, all stillness there. One could not help looking from one to the other. Meanwhile, since all the doors and windows were open in the heat, there was a perpetual sighing and ceasing sound, the voice of the transient and the perishing, it seemed, coming and going like human breath, while in the looking-glass things had ceased to breathe and lay still in the trance of immortality.

Half an hour ago the mistress of the house, Isabella Tyson, had gone down the grass path in her thin summer dress, carrying a basket, and had vanished, sliced off by the gilt rim of the looking-glass. She had gone presumably into the lower garden to pick flowers; or as it seemed more natural to suppose, to pick something light and fantastic and leafy and trailing, traveller's joy, or one of those elegant sprays of convolvulus that twine round ugly walls and burst here and there into white and violet blossoms. She suggested the fantastic and the tremulous convolvulus rather than the upright aster, the starched zinnia, or her own burning roses alight like lamps on the straight posts of their rose trees. The comparison showed how very little, after all these years, one knew about her; for it is impossible that any woman of flesh and blood of fifty-five or sixty should be really a wreath or a tendril. Such comparisons are worse than idle and superficial – they are cruel even, for they come like the convolvulus itself trembling between one's eyes and the truth. There must be truth; there must be a wall. Yet it was strange that after knowing her all these years one could not say what the truth about Isabella was; one still made up phrases like this about convolvulus and traveller's joy. As for facts, it was a fact that she

was a spinster; that she was rich; that she had bought
this house and collected with her own hands – often in
the most obscure corners of the world and at great risk
from poisonous stings and Oriental diseases – the rugs,
the chairs, the cabinets which now lived their nocturnal
life before one's eyes. Sometimes it seemed as if they
knew more about her than we, who sat on them, wrote
at them, and trod on them so carefully, were allowed to
know. In each of these cabinets were many little drawers, and each almost certainly held letters, tied with
bows of ribbon, sprinkled with sticks of lavender or
rose leaves. For it was another fact – if facts were what
one wanted – that Isabella had known many people,
had had many friends; and thus if one had the audacity
to open a drawer and read her letters, one would find
the traces of many agitations, of appointments to meet,
of upbraidings for not having met, long letters of
intimacy and affection, violent letters of jealousy and
reproach, terrible final words of parting – for all those
interviews and assignations had led to nothing – that
is, she had never married, and yet, judging from the
mask-like indifference of her face, she had gone through
twenty times more of passion and experience than
those whose loves are trumpeted forth for all the world
to hear. Under the stress of thinking about Isabella, her
room became more shadowy and symbolic; the corners

seemed darker, the legs of chairs and tables more spindly and hieroglyphic.

Suddenly these reflections were ended violently and yet without a sound. A large black form loomed into the looking-glass; blotted out everything, strewed the table with a packet of marble tablets veined with pink and grey, and was gone. But the picture was entirely altered. For the moment it was unrecognizable and irrational and entirely out of focus. One could not relate these tablets to any human purpose. And then by degrees some logical process set to work on them and began ordering and arranging them and bringing them into the fold of common experience. One realized at last that they were merely letters. The man had brought the post.

There they lay on the marble-topped table, all dripping with light and colour at first and crude and unabsorbed. And then it was strange to see how they were drawn in and arranged and composed and made part of the picture and granted that stillness and immortality which the looking-glass conferred. They lay there invested with a new reality and significance and with a greater heaviness, too, as if it would have needed a chisel to dislodge them from the table. And, whether it was fancy or not, they seemed to have become not merely a handful of casual letters but to be tablets graven with eternal truth – if one could read them, one would know everything there was to be known about Isabella, yes, and about life, too. The pages inside those marble-looking envelopes must be cut deep and scored thick with meaning. Isabella would come in, and take them, one by one, very slowly, and open them, and read them carefully word by word, and then with a profound sigh of comprehension, as if she had seen to the bottom of everything, she would tear the envelopes to little bits and tie the letters together and lock the cabinet drawer in her determination to conceal what she did not wish to be known.

The thought served as a challenge. Isabella did not wish to be known – but she should no longer escape. It was absurd, it was monstrous. If she concealed so much and knew so much one must prise her open with the first tool that came to hand – the imagination. One must fix one's mind upon her at that very moment. One must fasten her down there. One must refuse to be put off any longer with sayings and doings such as the moment brought forth – with dinners and visits and polite conver-sations. One must put oneself in her shoes. If one took the phrase literally, it was easy to see the shoes in which she stood, down in the lower garden, at this moment. They were very narrow and long and fashionable – they were made of the softest and most flexible leather. Like everything she wore, they were exquisite. And she would be standing under the high hedge in the lower part of the garden, raising the scissors that were tied to her waist to cut some dead flower, some overgrown branch. The sun would beat down on her face, into her eyes; but no, at the critical moment a veil of cloud covered the sun, making the expression of her eyes doubtful – was it mocking or tender, brilliant or dull? One could only see the indeterminate outline of her rather faded, fine face looking at the sky. She was thinking, perhaps, that she must order a new net for the strawberries; that she must send flowers to Johnson's widow; that it was time she drove over to see the Hippesleys in their new house. Those were the things she talked about at dinner certainly. But one was tired of the things that she talked about at dinner. It was her profounder state of being that one wanted to catch and turn to words, the state that is to the mind what breathing is to the body, what one calls happiness or unhappiness. At the mention of those words it became obvious, surely, that she must be happy. She was rich; she was distinguished; she had many friends; she travelled – she bought rugs in Turkey and blue pots in Persia. Avenues of pleasure radiated this way and that from where she stood with her scissors raised to cut the trembling branches while the lacy clouds veiled her face.

Here with a quick movement of her scissors she snipped the spray of traveller's joy and it fell to the ground. As it fell, surely some light came in too, surely one could penetrate a little farther into her being. Her mind then was filled with tenderness and regret . . . To cut an overgrown branch saddened her because it had once lived, and life was dear to her. Yes, and at the same time the fall of the branch would suggest to her how she must die herself and all the futility and evanescence of things. And then again quickly catching this thought up, with her instant good sense, she thought life had treated her well; even if fall she must, it was to lie on the earth and moulder sweetly into the roots of violets. So she stood thinking. Without making any thought precise – for she was one of those reticent people whose minds hold their thoughts enmeshed in clouds of silence – she was filled with thoughts. Her mind was like her room, in which lights advanced and retreated, came pirouetting and stepping delicately, spread their tails, pecked their way; and then her whole being was suffused, like the room again, with a cloud of some profound knowledge, some unspoken regret, and then she was full of locked drawers, stuffed with letters, like her cabinets. To talk of 'prising her open' as if she were an oyster, to use any but the finest and subtlest and most pliable tools upon her was impious and absurd.

A Society

This is how it all came about. Six or seven of us were sitting one day after tea. Some were gazing across the street into the windows of a milliner's shop where the light still shone brightly upon scarlet feathers and golden slippers. Others were idly occupied in building little towers of sugar upon the edge of the tea tray. After a time, so far as I can remember, we drew round the fire and began as usual to praise men – how strong, how noble, how brilliant, how courageous, how beautiful they were – how we envied those who by hook or by crook managed to get attached to one for life – when Poll, who had said nothing, burst into tears. Poll, I must tell you, has always been queer. For one thing her father was a strange man. He left her a fortune in his will, but on condition that she read all the books in the London Library. We comforted her as best we could; but we knew in our hearts how vain it was. For though we like her, Poll is no beauty; leaves her shoe laces untied; and must have been thinking, while we praised men, that not one of them would ever wish to marry her. At last she dried her tears. For some time we could make nothing of what she said. Strange enough it was in all conscience. She told us that, as we knew, she spent most of her time in the London Library, reading. She had begun, she said, with English literature on the top floor; and was steadily working her way down to *The Times* on the bottom. And now half, or perhaps only a quarter, way through a terrible thing had happened. She could read no more. Books were not what we thought them. 'Books,' she cried, rising to her feet and speaking with an intensity of desolation which I shall never forget, 'are for the most part unutterably bad!'

Of course we cried out that Shakespeare wrote books, and Milton and Shelley.

'Oh yes,' she interrupted us. 'You've been well taught, I can see. But you are not members of the London Library.' Here her sobs broke forth anew. At length, recovering a little, she opened one of the pile of books which she always carried about with her – 'From a Window' or 'In a Garden' or some such name as that it was called, and it was written by a man called Benton or Henson or something of that kind. She read the first few pages. We listened in silence. 'But that's not a book,' someone said. So she chose another. This time it was a history, but I have forgotten the writer's name. Our trepidation increased as she went on. Not a word of it seemed to be true, and the style in which it was written was execrable.

'Poetry! Poetry!' we cried, impatiently. 'Read us poetry!' I cannot describe the desolation which fell upon us as she opened a little volume and mouthed out the verbose, sentimental foolery which it contained.

'It must have been written by a woman,' one of us urged. But no. She told us that it was written by a young man, one of the most famous poets of the day. I leave you to imagine what the shock of the discovery was. Though we all cried and begged her to read no more she persisted and read us extracts from the *Lives of the Lord Chancellors*. When she had finished, Jane, the eldest and wisest of us, rose to her feet and said that she for one was not convinced.

'Why,' she asked, 'if men write such rubbish as this, should our mothers have wasted their youth in bringing them into the world?'

We were all silent; and in the silence, poor Poll could be heard sobbing out, 'Why, why did my father teach me to read?'

Clorinda was the first to come to her senses. 'It's all our fault,' she said. 'Every one of us knows how to read. But no one, save Poll, has ever taken the trouble to do it. I, for one, have taken it for granted that it was a woman's duty to spend her youth in bearing children. I venerated my mother for bearing ten; still more my grandmother for bearing fifteen; it was, I confess, my own ambition to bear twenty. We have gone on all these ages supposing that men were equally industrious, and that their works were of equal merit. While we have borne the children, they, we supposed, have borne the books and the pictures. We have populated the world. They have civilized it. But now that we can read, what prevents us from judging the results? Before we bring another child into the world we must swear that we will find out what the world is like.'

So we made ourselves into a society for asking questions. One of us was to visit a man-of-war; another was to hide herself in a scholar's study; another was to attend a meeting of business men; while all were to read books, look at pictures, go to concerts, keep our eyes open in the streets; and ask questions perpetually. We were very young. You can judge of our simplicity when I tell you that before parting that night we agreed that the objects of life were to produce good people and good books. Our questions were to be directed to finding out how far these objects were now attained by men. We vowed solemnly that we would not bear a single child until we were satisfied.

Off we went then, some to the British Museum; others to the King's Navy; some to Oxford; others to Cambridge; we visited the Royal Academy and the Tate; heard modern music in concert rooms, went to the Law Courts, and saw new plays. No one dined out without asking her partner certain questions and carefully noting his replies. At intervals we met together and compared our observations. Oh, those were merry meetings! Never have I laughed so much as I did when Rose read her notes upon 'Honour' and described how she had dressed herself as an Ethiopian Prince and gone aboard one of His Majesty's ships. Discovering the hoax, the Captain visited her (now disguised as a private gentleman) and demanded that honour should be satisfied. 'But how?' she asked. 'How?' he bellowed. 'With the cane of course!' Seeing that he was beside himself with rage and expecting that her last moment had come, she bent over and received, to her amazement, six light taps upon the behind. 'The honour of the British Navy is avenged!' he cried, and, raising herself, she saw him with the sweat pouring down his face holding out a trembling right hand. 'Away!' she exclaimed, striking an attitude and imitating the ferocity of his own expression, 'My honour has still to be satisfied!' 'Spoken like a gentleman!' he returned, and fell into profound thought. 'If six strokes avenge the honour of the King's

Navy,' he mused, 'how many avenge the honour of a private gentleman?' He said he would prefer to lay the case before his brother officers. She replied haughtily that she could not wait. He praised her sensibility. 'Let me see,' he cried suddenly, 'did your father keep a carriage?' 'No,' she said. 'Or a riding horse?' 'We had a donkey,' she bethought her, 'which drew the mowing machine.' At this his face lightened. 'My mother's name –' she added. 'For God's sake, man, don't mention your mother's name!' he shrieked, trembling like an aspen and flushing to the roots of his hair, and it was ten minutes at least before she could induce him to proceed. At length he decreed that if she gave him four strokes and a half in the small of the back at a spot indicated by himself (the half conceded, he said, in recognition of the fact that her great grandmother's uncle was killed at Trafalgar) it was his opinion that her honour would be as good as new. This was done; they retired to a restaurant; drank two bottles of wine for which he insisted upon paying; and parted with protestations of eternal friendship.

Then we had Fanny's account of her visit to the Law Courts. At her first visit she had come to the conclusion that the Judges were either made of wood or were impersonated by large animals resembling man who had been trained to move with extreme dignity, mumble and nod their heads. To test her theory she had liberated a handkerchief of bluebottles at the critical moment of a trial, but was unable to judge whether the creatures gave signs of humanity for the buzzing of the flies induced so sound a sleep that she only woke in time to see the prisoners led into the cells below. But from the evidence she brought we voted that it is unfair to suppose that the Judges are men.

Helen went to the Royal Academy, but when asked to deliver her report upon the pictures she began to recite from a pale blue volume, 'O for the touch of a vanished hand and the sound of a voice that is still. Home is the hunter, home from the hill. He gave his bridle reins a shake. Love is sweet, love is brief. Spring, the fair spring, is the year's pleasant King. O! to be in England now that April's there. Men must work and women must weep. The path of duty is the way to glory –' We could listen to no more of this gibberish.

'We want no more poetry!' we cried.

'Daughters of England!' she began, but here we pulled her down, a vase of water getting spilt over her in the scuffle.

'Thank God!' she exclaimed, shaking herself like a dog. 'Now I'll roll on the carpet and see if I can't brush off what remains of the Union Jack. Then perhaps –' here she rolled energetically. Getting up she began to explain to us what modern pictures are like when Castalia stopped her.

'What is the average size of a picture?' she asked. 'Perhaps two feet by two and a half,' she said. Castalia made notes while Helen spoke, and when she had done, and we were trying not to meet each other's eyes, rose and said, 'At your wish I spent last week at Oxbridge, disguised as a charwoman. I thus had access to the rooms of several Professors and will now attempt to give you some idea – only,' she broke off, 'I can't think how to do it. It's all so queer. These Professors,' she went on, 'live in large houses built round grass plots each in a kind of cell by himself. Yet they have every convenience and comfort. You have only to press a button or light a little lamp. Their papers are beautifully filed. Books abound. There are no children or animals, save half a dozen stray cats and one aged bullfinch – a cock. I remember,' she broke off, 'an Aunt of mine who lived at Dulwich and kept cactuses. You reached the conservatory through the double drawing-room, and there, on the hot pipes, were dozens of them, ugly, squat, bristly little plants each in a separate pot. Once in a hundred years the Aloe flowered, so my Aunt said. But she died before that happened –' We told her to keep to the point. 'Well,' she resumed, 'when Professor Hobkin was out I examined his life work, an edition of

Sappho. It's a queer-looking book, six or seven inches thick, not all by Sappho. Oh no. Most of it is a defence of Sappho's chastity, which some German had denied, and I can assure you the passion with which these two gentlemen argued, the learning they displayed, the prodigious ingenuity with which they disputed the use of some implement which looked to me for all the world like a hairpin astounded me; especially when the door opened and Professor Hobkin himself appeared. A very nice, mild, old gentleman, but what could *he* know about chastity?' We misunderstood her.

'No, no,' she protested, 'he's the soul of honour I'm sure – not that he resembles Rose's sea captain in the least. I was thinking rather of my Aunt's cactuses. What could *they* know about chastity?'

Again we told her not to wander from the point – did the Oxbridge professors help to produce good people and good books? – the objects of life.

'There!' she exclaimed. 'It never struck me to ask. It never occurred to me that they could possibly produce anything.'

'I believe,' said Sue, 'that you made some mistake. Probably Professor Hobkin was a gynæcologist. A scholar is a very different sort of man. A scholar is overflowing with humour and invention – perhaps addicted to wine, but what of that? – a delightful companion, generous, subtle, imaginative – as stands to reason. For he spends his life in company with the finest human beings that have ever existed.'

'Hum,' said Castalia. 'Perhaps I'd better go back and try again.'

Some three months later it happened that I was sitting alone when Castalia entered. I don't know what it was in the look of her that so moved me; but I could not restrain myself, and dashing across the room, I clasped her in my arms. Not only was she very beautiful; she seemed also in the highest spirits. 'How happy you look!' I exclaimed, as she sat down.

'I've been at Oxbridge,' she said.

'Asking questions?'

'Answering them,' she replied.

'You have not broken our vow?' I said anxiously, noticing something about her figure.

'Oh, the vow,' she said casually. 'I'm going to have a baby if that's what you mean. You can't imagine,' she burst out, 'how exciting, how beautiful, how satisfying –'

'What is?' I asked.

'To – to – answer questions,' she replied in some confusion. Whereupon she told me the whole of her story. But in the middle of an account which interested and excited me more than anything I had ever heard, she gave the strangest cry, half whoop, half holloa –

'Chastity! Chastity! Where's my chastity!' she cried. 'Help Ho! The scent bottle!'

There was nothing in the room but a cruet containing mustard, which I was about to administer when she recovered her composure.

'You should have thought of that three months ago,' I said severely.

'True,' she replied. 'There's not much good in thinking of it now. It was unfortunate, by the way, that my mother had me called Castalia.'

'Oh Castalia, your mother –' I was beginning when she reached for the mustard pot.

'No, no, no,' she said, shaking her head. 'If you'd been a chaste woman yourself you would have screamed at the sight of me – instead of which you rushed across the room and took me in your arms. No, Cassandra. We are neither of us chaste.' So we went on talking.

Meanwhile the room was filling up, for it was the day appointed to discuss the results of our observations. Everyone, I thought, felt as I did about Castalia. They kissed her and said how glad they were to see her again. At length, when we were all assembled, Jane rose and said that it was time to begin. She began by saying that we had now asked questions for over five years, and that though the results were bound to be inconclusive – here Castalia nudged me and whispered that she was not so sure about that. Then she got up, and, interrupting Jane in the middle of a sentence, said,

'Before you say any more, I want to know – am I to stay in the room? Because,' she added, 'I have to confess that I am an impure woman.'

Everyone looked at her in astonishment.

'You are going to have a baby?' asked Jane.

She nodded her head.

It was extraordinary to see the different expressions on their faces. A sort of hum went through the room, in which I could catch the words 'impure', 'baby', 'Castalia', and so on. Jane, who was herself considerably moved, put it to us,

'Shall she go? Is she impure?'

Such a roar filled the room as might have been heard in the street outside.

'No! No! No! Let her stay! Impure? Fiddlesticks!' Yet I fancied that some of the youngest, girls of nineteen or twenty, held back as if overcome with shyness. Then we all came about her and began asking questions, and at last I saw one of the youngest, who had kept in the background, approach shyly and say to her:

'What is chastity then? I mean is it good, or is it bad, or is it nothing at all?' She replied so low that I could not catch what she said.

'You know I was shocked,' said another, 'for at least ten minutes.'

'In my opinion,' said Poll, who was growing crusty from always reading in the London Library, 'chastity is nothing but ignorance – a most discreditable state of mind. We should admit only the unchaste to our society. I vote that Castalia shall be our President.'

This was violently disputed.

'It is as unfair to brand women with chastity as with unchastity,' said Moll. 'Some of us haven't the opportunity either. Moreover, I don't believe Cassy herself maintains that she acted as she did from a pure love of knowledge.'

'He is only twenty-one and divinely beautiful,' said Cassy, with a ravishing gesture.

'I move,' said Helen, 'that no one be allowed to talk of chastity or unchastity save those who are in love.'

'Oh bother,' said Judith, who had been enquiring into scientific matters, 'I'm not in love and I'm longing to explain my measures for dispensing with prostitutes and fertilizing virgins by Act of Parliament.'

She went on to tell us of an invention of hers to be erected at Tube Stations and other public resorts, which, upon payment of a small fee would safeguard the nation's health, accommodate its sons, and relieve its

daughters. Then she had contrived a method of pre-
serving in sealed tubes the germs of future Lord
Chancellors 'or poets or painters or musicians' she went
on, 'supposing, that is to say, that these breeds are not
extinct, and that women still wish to bear children —'

'Of course we wish to bear children!' cried Castalia
impatiently. Jane rapped the table.

'That is the very point we are met to consider,' she
said. 'For five years we have been trying to find out
whether we are justified in continuing the human race.
Castalia has anticipated our decision. But it remains for
the rest of us to make up our minds.'

Here one after another of our messengers rose and
delivered their reports. The marvels of civilization far
exceeded our expectations, and as we learnt for the first
time how man flies in the air, talks across space, pene-
trates to the heart of an atom, and embraces the
universe in his speculations a murmur of admiration
burst from our lips.

'We are proud,' we cried, 'that our mothers sacrificed
their youth in such a cause as this!' Castalia, who had
been listening intently, looked prouder than all the rest.
Then Jane reminded us that we had still much to learn,
and Castalia begged us to make haste. On we went
through a vast tangle of statistics. We learnt that England
has a population of so many millions, and that such and

such a proportion of them is constantly hungry and in prison; that the average size of a working man's family is such, and that so great a percentage of women die from maladies incident to childbirth. Reports were read of visits to factories, shops, slums, and dockyards. Descriptions were given of the Stock Exchange, of a gigantic house of business in the City, and of a Government Office. The British Colonies were now discussed, and some account was given of our rule in India, Africa and Ireland. I was sitting by Castalia and I noticed her uneasiness.

'We shall never come to any conclusion at all at this rate,' she said. 'As it appears that civilization is so much more complex than we had any notion, would it not be better to confine ourselves to our original enquiry? We agreed that it was the object of life to produce good people and good books. All this time we have been talking of aeroplanes, factories and money. Let us talk about men themselves and their arts, for that is the heart of the matter.'

So the diners-out stepped forward with long slips of paper containing answers to their questions. These had been framed after much consideration. A good man, we had agreed, must at any rate be honest, passionate, and unworldly. But whether or not a particular man possessed those qualities could only be discovered by asking questions, often beginning at a remote distance from the centre. Is Kensington a nice place to live in? Where is your son being educated – and your daughter? Now please tell me, what do you pay for your cigars? By the way, is Sir Joseph a baronet or only a knight? Often it seemed that we learnt more from trivial questions of this kind than from more direct ones. 'I accepted my peerage,' said Lord Bunkum, 'because my wife wished it.' I forget how many titles were accepted for the same reason. 'Working fifteen hours out of the twenty-four as I do –' ten thousand professional men began.

'No, no, of course you can neither read nor write. But why do you work so hard?' 'My dear lady, with a growing family –' 'But *why* does your family grow?' Their wives wished that too, or perhaps it was the British Empire. But more significant than the answers were the refusals to answer. Very few would reply at all to questions about morality and religion, and such answers as were given were not serious. Questions as to the value of money and power were almost invariably brushed aside, or pressed at extreme risk to the asker. 'I'm sure,' said Jill, 'that if Sir Harley Tightboots hadn't been carving the mutton when I asked him about the capitalist system he would have cut my throat. The only reason why we escaped with our lives over and over again is that men are at once so hungry and so chivalrous. They despise us too much to mind what we say.'

'Of course they despise us,' said Eleanor. 'At the same time how do you account for this – I made enquiries among the artists. Now no woman has ever been an artist, has she, Poll?'

'Jane-Austen-Charlotte-Brontë-George-Eliot,' cried Poll, like a man crying muffins in a back street.

'Damn the woman!' someone exclaimed. 'What a bore she is!'

'Since Sappho there has been no female of first rate –' Eleanor began, quoting from a weekly newspaper.

'It's now well known that Sappho was the somewhat lewd invention of Professor Hobkin,' Ruth interrupted.

'Anyhow, there is no reason to suppose that any woman ever has been able to write or ever will be able to write,' Eleanor continued. 'And yet, whenever I go among authors they never cease to talk to me about their books. Masterly! I say, or Shakespeare himself! (for one must say something) and I assure you, they believe me.'

'That proves nothing,' said Jane. 'They all do it. Only,' she sighed, 'it doesn't seem to help *us* much. Perhaps we had better examine modern literature next. Liz, it's your turn.'

Elizabeth rose and said that in order to prosecute her enquiry she had dressed as a man and been taken for a reviewer.

'I have read new books pretty steadily for the past

five years,' said she. 'Mr Wells is the most popular living writer; then comes Mr Arnold Bennett; then Mr Compton Mackenzie; Mr McKenna and Mr Walpole may be bracketed together.' She sat down.

'But you've told us nothing!' we expostulated. 'Or do you mean that these gentlemen have greatly surpassed Jane-Eliot and that English fiction is – where's that review of yours? Oh, yes, "safe in their hands".'

'Safe, quite safe,' she said, shifting uneasily from foot to foot. 'And I'm sure that they give away even more than they receive.'

We were all sure of that. 'But,' we pressed her, 'do they write good books?'

'Good books?' she said, looking at the ceiling. 'You must remember,' she began, speaking with extreme rapidity, 'that fiction is the mirror of life. And you can't deny that education is of the highest importance, and that it would be extremely annoying, if you found yourself alone at Brighton late at night, not to know which was the best boarding house to stay at, and suppose it was a dripping Sunday evening – wouldn't it be nice to go to the Movies?'

'But what has that got to do with it?' we asked.

'Nothing – nothing – nothing whatever,' she replied.

'Well, tell us the truth,' we bade her.

'The truth? But isn't it wonderful,' she broke off –

'Mr Chitter has written a weekly article for the past thirty years upon love or hot buttered toast and has sent all his sons to Eton –'

'The truth!' we demanded.

'Oh the truth,' she stammered – 'the truth has nothing to do with literature,' and sitting down she refused to say another word.

It all seemed to us very inconclusive.

'Ladies, we must try to sum up the results,' Jane was beginning, when a hum, which had been heard for some time through the open window, drowned her voice.

'War! War! War! Declaration of War!' men were shouting in the street below.

We looked at each other in horror.

'What war?' we cried. 'What war?' We remembered, too late, that we had never thought of sending anyone to the House of Commons. We had forgotten all about it. We turned to Poll, who had reached the history shelves in the London Library, and asked her to enlighten us.

'Why,' we cried, 'do men go to war?'

'Sometimes for one reason, sometimes for another,' she replied calmly. 'In 1760, for example –' The shouts outside drowned her words. 'Again in 1797 – in 1804 – It was the Austrians in 1866 – 1870 was the Franco-Prussian – In 1900 on the other hand –'

'But it's now 1914!' we cut her short.

'Ah, I don't know what they're going to war for now,' she admitted.

The war was over and peace was in process of being signed when I once more found myself with Castalia in the room where our meetings used to be held. We began idly turning over the pages of our old minute books. 'Queer,' I mused, 'to see what we were thinking five years ago.' 'We are agreed,' Castalia quoted, reading over my shoulder, 'that it is the object of life to produce good people and good books.' We made no comment upon that. 'A good man is at any rate honest, passionate and unworldly.' 'What a woman's language,' I observed. 'Oh dear,' cried Castalia, pushing the book away from her, 'What fools we were! It was all Poll's father's fault,' she went on. 'I believe he did it on purpose – that ridiculous will, I mean, forcing Poll to read all the books in the London Library. If we hadn't learnt to read,' she said bitterly, 'we might still have been bearing children in ignorance and that I believe was the happiest life after all. I know what you're going to say about war,' she checked me, 'and the horror of bearing children to see them killed, but our mothers did it, and their mothers, and their mothers before them. And *they* didn't complain. They couldn't read. I've done my best,' she sighed, 'to prevent my little girl from learning to read, but what's the use? I caught Ann only yesterday with a newspaper in her hand and she was beginning to ask me if it was "true". Next she'll ask me whether Mr Lloyd George is a good man, then whether Mr Arnold Bennett is a good novelist, and finally whether I believe in God. How can I bring my daughter up to believe in nothing?' she demanded.

'Surely you could teach her to believe that a man's intellect is, and always will be, fundamentally superior to a woman's?' I suggested. She brightened at this and began to turn over our old minutes again. 'Yes,' she said, 'think of their discoveries, their mathematics, their science, their philosophy, their scholarship –' and then she began to laugh, 'I shall never forget old Hobkin and the hairpin,' she said, and went on reading and laughing and I thought she was quite happy, when suddenly she threw the book from her and burst out, 'Oh, Cassandra why do you torment me? Don't you know that our belief in man's intellect is the greatest fallacy of them all?' 'What?' I exclaimed. 'Ask any journalist, schoolmaster, politician or public-house keeper in the land and they will all tell you that men are much cleverer than women.' 'As if I doubted it,' she said scornfully. 'How could they help it? Haven't we bred them and fed and kept them in comfort since the beginning of time so that they may be clever even if they're nothing else? It's all our doing!' she cried. 'We insisted upon having intellect and now we've got it. And it's intellect,' she continued, 'that's at the bottom of it. What could be more charming than a boy before he has begun to cultivate his intellect? He is beautiful to look at; he gives himself no airs; he understands the meaning of art and literature instinctively; he goes about enjoying his life and making other people enjoy theirs. Then they teach him to cultivate his intellect. He becomes a barrister, a civil servant, a general, an author, a professor. Every day he goes to an office. Every year he produces a book. He maintains a whole family by the products of his brain – poor devil! Soon he cannot come into a room without making us all feel uncomfortable; he condescends to every woman he meets, and dares not tell the truth even to his own wife; instead of rejoicing our eyes we have to shut them if we are to take him in our arms. True, they console themselves with stars of all shapes, ribbons of all shades, and incomes of all sizes – but what is to console us? That we shall be able in ten years' time to spend a week-end at Lahore? Or that the least insect in Japan has a name twice the length of its body? Oh, Cassandra, for Heaven's sake let us devise a method by which men may bear children! It is our only chance. For unless we provide them with some innocent occupation we shall get neither good people nor good books; we shall perish beneath the fruits of their unbridled activity; and not a human being will survive to know that there once was Shakespeare!'

'It is too late,' I said. 'We cannot provide even for the children that we have.'

'And then you ask me to believe in intellect,' she said.

While we spoke, men were crying hoarsely and wearily in the street, and listening, we heard that the Treaty of Peace had just been signed. The voices died away. The rain was falling and interfered no doubt with the proper explosion of the fireworks.

'My cook will have bought the *Evening News*,' said Castalia, 'and Ann will be spelling it out over her tea. I must go home.'

'It's no good – not a bit of good,' I said. 'Once she knows how to read there's only one thing you can teach her to believe in – and that is herself.'

'Well, that would be a change,' said Castalia.

So we swept up the papers of our Society, and though Ann was playing with her doll very happily, we solemnly made her a present of the lot and told her we had chosen her to be President of the Society of the future – upon which she burst into tears, poor little girl.

The Mark on the Wall

Perhaps it was the middle of January in the present year that I first looked up and saw the mark on the wall. In order to fix a date it is necessary to remember what one saw. So now I think of the fire; the steady film of yellow light upon the page of my book; the three chrysanthemums in the round glass bowl on the mantelpiece. Yes, it must have been the winter time, and we had just finished our tea, for I remember that I was smoking a cigarette when I looked up and saw the mark on the wall for the first time. I looked up through the smoke of my cigarette and my eye lodged for a moment upon the burning coals, and that old fancy of the crimson flag flapping from the castle tower came into my mind, and I thought of the cavalcade of red knights riding up the side of the black rock. Rather to my relief the sight of the mark interrupted the fancy, for it is an old fancy, an automatic fancy, made as a child perhaps. The mark was a small round mark, black upon the white wall, about six or seven inches above the mantelpiece.

How readily our thoughts swarm upon a new object, lifting it a little way, as ants carry a blade of straw so feverishly, and then leave it . . . If that mark was made by a nail, it can't have been for a picture, it must have been for a miniature – the miniature of a lady with white powdered curls, powder-dusted cheeks, and lips like red carnations. A fraud of course, for the people who had this house before us would have chosen pictures in that way – an old picture for an old room. That is the sort of people they were – very interesting people, and I think of them so often, in such queer places, because one will never see them again, never know what happened next. They wanted to leave this house because they wanted to change their style of furniture, so he said, and he was in process of saying that in his opinion art should have ideas behind it when we were torn asunder, as one is torn from the old lady about to pour out tea and the young man about to hit the tennis ball in the back garden of the suburban villa as one rushes past in the train.

But as for that mark, I'm not sure about it; I don't believe it was made by a nail after all; it's too big, too round, for that. I might get up, but if I got up and looked at it, ten to one I shouldn't be able to say for certain;

because once a thing's done, no one ever knows how it happened. O dear me, the mystery of life! The inaccuracy of thought! The ignorance of humanity! To show how very little control of our possessions we have – what an accidental affair this living is after all our civilization – let me just count over a few of the things lost in one lifetime, beginning, for that seems always the most mysterious of losses – what cat would gnaw, what rat would nibble – three pale blue canisters of book-binding tools? Then there were the bird cages, the iron hoops, the steel skates, the Queen Anne coal-scuttle, the bagatelle board, the hand organ – all gone, and jewels too. Opals and emeralds, they lie about the roots of turnips. What a scraping paring affair it is to be sure! The wonder is that I've any clothes on my back, that I sit surrounded by solid furniture at this moment. Why, if one wants to compare life to anything, one must liken it to being blown through the Tube at fifty miles an hour – landing at the other end without a single hairpin in one's hair! Shot out at the feet of God entirely naked! Tumbling head over heels in the asphodel meadows like brown-paper parcels pitched down a shoot in the post office! With one's hair flying back like the tail of a race-horse. Yes, that seems to express the rapidity of life, the perpetual waste and repair; all so casual, all so haphazard . . .

But after life. The slow pulling down of thick green stalks so that the cup of the flower, as it turns over, deluges one with purple and red light. Why, after all, should one not be born there as one is born here, helpless, speechless, unable to focus one's eyesight, groping at the roots of the grass, at the toes of the Giants? As for saying which are trees, and which are men and women, or whether there are such things, that one won't be in a condition to do for fifty years or so. There will be nothing but spaces of light and dark, intersected by thick stalks, and rather higher up perhaps, rose-shaped blots of an indistinct colour – dim pinks and blues – which will, as time goes on, become more definite, become – I don't know what . . .

And yet that mark on the wall is not a hole at all. It may even be caused by some round black substance, such as a small rose leaf, left over from the summer, and I, not being a very vigilant housekeeper – look at the dust on the mantelpiece, for example, the dust which, so they say, buried Troy three times over, only fragments of pots utterly refusing annihilation, as one can believe.

The tree outside the window taps very gently on the pane . . . I want to think quietly, calmly, spaciously, never to be interrupted, never to have to rise from my chair, to slip easily from one thing to another, without any sense of hostility, or obstacle. I want to sink deeper and deeper, away from the surface, with its hard separate facts. To steady myself, let me catch hold of the first idea that passes . . . Shakespeare . . . Well, he will do as well as another. A man who sat himself solidly in an arm-chair, and looked into the fire so – A shower of ideas fell perpetually from some very high Heaven down through his mind. He leant his forehead on his hand, and people, looking in through the open door – for this scene is supposed to take place on a summer's evening – But how dull this is, this historical fiction! It doesn't interest me at all. I wish I could hit upon a pleasant track of thought, a track indirectly reflecting credit upon myself, for those are the pleasantest thoughts, and very frequent even in the minds of modest mouse-coloured people, who believe genuinely that they dislike to hear their own praises. They are not thoughts directly praising oneself; that is the beauty of them; they are thoughts like this:

'And then I came into the room. They were discussing botany. I said how I'd seen a flower growing on a dust heap on the site of an old house in Kingsway. The seed, I said, must have been sown in the reign of Charles the First. 'What flowers grew in the reign of Charles the First?' I asked – (but I don't remember the answer). Tall flowers with purple tassels to them perhaps. And so it goes on. All the time I'm dressing up the figure of myself in my own mind, lovingly, stealthily, not openly adoring it, for if I did that, I should catch myself out, and stretch my hand at once for a book in self-protection. Indeed, it is curious how instinctively one protects the image of oneself from idolatry or any other handling that could make it ridiculous, or too unlike the original to be believed in any longer. Or is it not so very curious after all? It is a matter of great importance. Suppose the looking-glass smashes, the image disappears, and the romantic figure with the green of forest depths all about it is there no longer, but only that shell of a person which is seen by other people – what an airless, shallow, bald, prominent world it becomes! A world not to be lived in. As we face each other in omnibuses and underground railways we are looking into the mirror; that accounts for the vagueness, the gleam of glassiness, in our eyes. And the novelists in future will realize more and more the importance of these reflections, for of course there is not one reflection but an almost infinite number; those are the depths they will explore, those the phantoms they will pursue, leaving the description of reality more and more out of their stories, taking a knowledge of it for granted, as the Greeks did and Shakespeare perhaps – but these generalizations are very worthless. The military sound of the word is enough. It recalls leading articles, cabinet ministers – a whole class of things indeed which as a child one thought the thing itself, the standard thing, the real thing, from which one could not depart save at the risk of nameless damnation. Generalizations bring back somehow Sunday in London, Sunday afternoon walks, Sunday luncheons, and also ways of speaking of the dead, clothes, and habits – like the habit of sitting all together in one room until a certain hour, although nobody liked it. There was a rule for everything. The rule for tablecloths at that particular period was that they should be made of tapestry with little yellow compartments marked upon them, such as you may see in photographs of the carpets in the corridors of the royal palaces. Tablecloths of a different kind were not real tablecloths. How shocking, and yet how wonderful it was to discover that these real things, Sunday luncheons, Sunday walks, country houses, and tablecloths were not entirely real, were indeed half phantoms, and the damnation which visited the disbeliever in them was only a sense of illegitimate freedom. What now takes the place of those things I wonder, those real standard things? Men perhaps, should you be a woman; the masculine point of view which governs our lives, which sets the standard, which establishes Whitaker's Table of Precedency, which has become, I suppose, since the war half a phantom to many men and women, which soon, one may hope, will be laughed into the dustbin where the phantoms go, the mahogany sideboards and the Landseer prints, Gods and Devils, Hell and so forth, leaving us all with an intoxicating sense of illegitimate freedom – if freedom exists . . .

In certain lights that mark on the wall seems actually to project from the wall. Nor is it entirely circular. I cannot be sure, but it seems to cast a perceptible shadow, suggesting that if I ran my finger down that strip of the wall it would, at a certain point, mount and descend a small tumulus, a smooth tumulus like those barrows on the South Downs which are, they say, either tombs or camps. Of the two I should prefer them to be tombs, desiring melancholy like most English people, and finding it natural at the end of a walk to think of the bones stretched beneath the turf . . . There must be some book about it. Some antiquary must have dug up those bones and given them a name . . . What sort of a man is an antiquary, I wonder? Retired Colonels for the most part, I daresay, leading parties of aged labourers to the top here, examining clods of earth and stone, and getting into correspondence with the neighbouring clergy, which, being opened at breakfast time, gives them a feeling of importance, and the comparison of arrowheads necessitates cross-country journeys to the county towns, an agreeable necessity both to them and to their elderly wives, who wish to make plum jam or to clean out the study, and have every reason for keeping that great question of the camp or the tomb in perpetual suspension, while the Colonel himself feels agreeably philosophic in accumulating evidence on both sides of the question. It is true that he does finally incline to believe in the camp; and, being opposed, indites a pamphlet which he is about to read at the quarterly meeting of the local society when a stroke lays him low, and his last conscious thoughts are not of wife or child, but of the camp and that arrow-head there, which is now in the case at the local museum, together with the foot of a Chinese murderess, a handful of Elizabethan nails, a great many Tudor clay pipes, a piece of Roman pottery, and the wine-glass that Nelson drank out of – proving I really don't know what.

No, no, nothing is proved, nothing is known. And if I were to get up at this very moment and ascertain that the mark on the wall is really – what shall we say? – the head of a gigantic old nail, driven in two hundred years ago, which has now, owing to the patient attrition of many generations of housemaids, revealed its head above the coat of paint, and is taking its first view of modern life in the sight of a white-walled fire-lit room, what should I gain? – Knowledge? Matter for further speculation? I can think sitting still as well as standing up. And what is knowledge? What are our learned men save the descendants of witches and hermits who crouched in caves and in woods brewing herbs, interrogating shrew-mice and writing down the language of the stars? And the less we honour them as our superstitions dwindle and our respect for beauty and health of mind increases . . . Yes, one could imagine a very pleasant world. A quiet spacious world, with the flowers so red and blue in the open fields. A world without professors or specialists or housekeepers with the profiles of policemen, a world which one could slice with one's thought as a fish slices the water with his fin, grazing the stems of the water-lilies, hanging suspended over nests of white sea eggs . . . How peaceful it is down here, rooted in the centre of the world and gazing up through the grey waters, with their sudden gleams of light, and their reflections – If it were not for Whitaker's Almanack – if it were not for the Table of Precedency!

I must jump up and see for myself what that mark on the wall really is – a nail, a rose-leaf, a crack in the wood?

Here is Nature once more at her old game of self-preservation. This train of thought, she perceives, is threatening mere waste of energy, even some collision with reality, for who will ever be able to lift a finger against Whitaker's Table of Precedency? The Archbishop of Canterbury is followed by the Lord High Chancellor; the Lord High Chancellor is followed by the Archbishop of York. Everybody follows somebody, such is the philosophy of Whitaker; and the great thing is to know who follows whom. Whitaker knows, and let that, so Nature counsels, comfort you, instead of enraging you; and if you can't be comforted, if you must shatter this hour of peace, think of the mark on the wall.

I understand Nature's game – her prompting to take action as a way of ending any thought that threatens to excite or to pain. Hence, I suppose, comes our slight contempt for men of action – men, we assume, who don't think. Still, there's no harm in putting a full stop to one's disagreeable thoughts by looking at a mark on the wall.

Indeed, now that I have fixed my eyes upon it, I feel that I have grasped a plank in the sea; I feel a satisfying sense of reality which at once turns the two Archbishops and the Lord High Chancellor to the shadows of shades. Here is something definite, something real. Thus, waking from a midnight dream of horror, one hastily turns on the light and lies quiescent, worshipping the chest of drawers, worshipping solidity, worshipping reality, worshipping the impersonal world which is a proof of some existence other than ours. That is what one wants to be sure of ... Wood is a pleasant thing to think about. It comes from a tree; and trees grow, and we don't know how they grow. For years and years they grow, without paying any attention to us, in meadows, in forests, and by the side of rivers – all things one likes to think about. The cows swish their tails beneath them on hot afternoons; they paint rivers so green that when a moorhen dives one expects to see its feathers all green when it comes up again. I like to think of the fish balanced against the stream like flags blown out; and of water-beetles slowly raising domes of mud upon the bed of the river. I like to think of the tree itself: first the close dry sensation of being wood; then the grinding of the storm; then the slow, delicious ooze of sap. I like to think of it, too, on winter's nights standing in the empty field with all leaves close-furled, nothing tender exposed to the iron bullets of the moon, a naked mast upon an earth that goes tumbling, tumbling, all night long. The song of birds must sound very loud and strange in June; and how cold the feet of insects must feel upon it, as they make laborious progresses up the creases of the bark, or sun themselves upon the thin green awning of the leaves, and look straight in front of them with diamond-cut red eyes ... One by one the fibres snap beneath the immense cold pressure of the earth, then the last storm comes and, falling, the highest branches drive deep into the ground again. Even so, life isn't done with; there are a million patient, watchful lives still for a tree, all over the world, in bedrooms, in ships, on the pavement, lining rooms where men and women sit after tea, smoking cigarettes. It is full of peaceful thoughts, happy thoughts, this tree. I should like to take each one separately – but something is getting in the way . . . Where was I? What has it all been about? A tree? A river? The Downs? Whitaker's Almanack? The fields of asphodel? I can't remember a thing. Everything's moving, falling, slipping, vanishing . . . There is a vast upheaval of matter. Someone is standing over me and saying –

'I'm going out to buy a newspaper.'

'Yes?'

'Though it's no good buying newspapers . . . Nothing ever happens. Curse this war! God damn this war! . . . All the same, I don't see why we should have a snail on our wall.'

Ah, the mark on the wall! It was a snail.

Solid Objects

The only thing that moved upon the vast semi-circle of the beach was one small black spot. As it came nearer to the ribs and spine of the stranded pilchard boat, it became apparent from a certain tenuity in its blackness that this spot possessed four legs; and moment by moment it became more unmistakable that it was composed of the persons of two young men. Even thus in outline against the sand there was an unmistakable vitality in them; an indescribable vigour in the approach and withdrawal of the bodies, slight though it was, which proclaimed some violent argument issuing from the tiny mouths of the little round heads. This was corroborated on closer view by the repeated lunging of a walking-stick on the right-hand side. 'You mean to tell me . . . You actually believe . . .' thus the walking-stick on the right-hand side next the waves seemed to be asserting as it cut long straight stripes upon the sand.

'Politics be damned!' issued clearly from the body on the left-hand side, and, as these words were uttered, the mouths, noses, chins, little moustaches, tweed caps, rough boots, shooting coats, and check stockings of the two speakers became clearer and clearer; the smoke of their pipes went up into the air; nothing was so solid, so living, so hard, red, hirsute and virile as these two bodies for miles and miles of sea and sandhill.

They flung themselves down by the six ribs and spine of the black pilchard boat. You know how the body seems to shake itself free from an argument, and to apologize for a mood of exaltation; flinging itself down and expressing in the looseness of its attitude a readiness to take up with something new – whatever it may be that comes next to hand. So Charles, whose stick had been slashing the beach for half a mile or so, began skimming flat pieces of slate over the water; and John, who had exclaimed 'Politics be damned!' began burrowing his fingers down, down, into the sand. As his hand went further and further beyond the wrist, so that he had to hitch his sleeve a little higher, his eyes lost their intensity, or rather the background of thought and experience which gives an inscrutable depth to the eyes of grown people disappeared, leaving only the clear transparent surface, expressing nothing but wonder, which the eyes of young children display. No doubt the act of burrowing in the sand had something to do with it. He remembered that, after digging for a little, the water oozes round your finger-tips; the hole then becomes a moat; a well; a spring; a secret channel to the sea. As he was choosing which of these things to make it, still working his fingers in the water, they curled round something hard – a full drop of solid matter – and gradually dislodged a large irregular lump, and brought it to the surface. When the sand coating was wiped off, a green tint appeared. It was a lump of glass, so thick as to be almost opaque; the smoothing of the sea had completely worn off any edge or shape, so that it was impossible to say whether it had been bottle, tumbler or window-pane; it was nothing but glass; it was almost a precious stone. You had only to enclose it in a rim of gold, or pierce it with a wire, and it became a jewel; part of a necklace, or a dull, green light upon a finger. Perhaps after all it was really a gem; something worn by a dark Princess trailing her finger in the water as she sat in the stern of the boat and listened to the slaves singing as they rowed her across the Bay. Or the oak sides of a sunk Elizabethan treasure-chest had split apart, and, rolled over and over, over and over, its emeralds had come at last to shore. John turned it in his hands; he held it to the light; he held it so that its irregular mass blotted out the body and extended right arm of his friend. The green thinned and thickened slightly as it was held against the sky or against the body. It pleased him; it puzzled him; it was so hard, so concentrated, so definite an object compared with the vague sea and the hazy shore.

Now a sigh disturbed him – profound, final, making him aware that his friend Charles had thrown all the flat stones within reach, or had come to the conclusion that it was not worth while to throw them. They ate their sandwiches side by side. When they had done, and were shaking themselves and rising to their feet, John took the lump of glass and looked at it in silence. Charles looked at it too. But he saw immediately that it was not flat, and filling his pipe he said with the energy that dismisses a foolish strain of thought,

'To return to what I was saying –'

He did not see, or if he had seen would hardly have noticed, that John after looking at the lump for a moment, as if in hesitation, slipped it inside his pocket. That impulse, too, may have been the impulse which leads a child to pick up one pebble on a path strewn with them, promising it a life of warmth and security upon the nursery mantelpiece, delighting in the sense of power and benignity which such an action confers, and believing that the heart of the stone leaps with joy when it sees itself chosen from a million like it, to enjoy this bliss instead of a life of cold and wet upon the high road. 'It might so easily have been any other of the millions of stones, but it was I, I, I!'

Whether this thought or not was in John's mind: the lump of glass had its place upon the mantelpiece, where it stood heavy upon a little pile of bills and letters, and served not only as an excellent paper-weight, but also as a natural stopping place for the young man's eyes when they wandered from his book. Looked at again and again half consciously by a mind thinking of something else, any object mixes itself so profoundly with the stuff of thought that it loses its actual form and recomposes itself a little differently in an ideal shape which haunts the brain when we least expect it. So John found himself attracted to the windows of curiosity shops when he was out walking, merely because he saw something which reminded him of the lump of glass. Anything, so long as it was an object of some kind, more or less round, perhaps with a dying flame deep sunk in its mass, anything – china, glass, amber, rock, marble – even the smooth oval egg of a prehistoric bird would do. He took, also, to keeping his eyes upon the ground, especially in the neighbourhood of waste land where the household refuse is thrown away. Such objects often occurred there – thrown away, of no use to anybody, shapeless, discarded. In a few months he had collected four or five specimens that took their place upon the mantelpiece. They were useful, too, for a man who is standing for Parliament upon the brink of a brilliant career has any number of papers to keep in order – addresses to constituents, declarations of policy, appeals for subscriptions, invitations to dinner, and so on.

One day, starting from his rooms in the Temple to catch a train in order to address his constituents, his eyes rested upon a remarkable object lying half-hidden in one of those little borders of grass which edge the bases of vast legal buildings. He could only touch it with the point of his stick through the railings; but he could see that it was a piece of china of the most remarkable shape, as nearly resembling a starfish as anything – shaped, or broken accidentally, into five irregular but unmistakable points. The colouring was mainly blue, but green stripes or spots of some kind overlaid the blue, and lines of crimson gave it a richness and lustre of the most attractive kind. John was determined to possess it; but the more he pushed, the further it receded. At length he was forced to go back to his rooms and improvise a wire ring attached to the end of a stick, with which, by dint of great care and skill, he finally drew the piece of china within reach of his hands. As he seized hold of it he exclaimed in triumph. At that moment the clock struck. It was out of the question that he should keep his appointment. The meeting was held without him. But how had the piece of china been broken into this remarkable shape? A careful examination put it beyond doubt that the star shape was accidental, which made it all the more strange, and it seemed unlikely that there should be another such in existence. Set at the opposite end of the mantelpiece from the lump of glass that had been dug from the sand, it looked like a creature from another world – freakish and fantastic as a harlequin. It seemed to be pirouetting through space; winking light like a fitful star. The contrast between the china so vivid and alert, and the glass so mute and contemplative, fascinated him, and wondering and amazed he asked himself how the two came to exist in the same world, let alone to stand upon the same narrow strip of marble in the same room. The question remained unanswered.

He now began to haunt the places which are most prolific of broken china, such as pieces of waste land between railway lines, sites of demolished houses, and commons in the neighbourhood of London. But china is seldom thrown from a great height; it is one of the rarest of human actions. You have to find in conjunction a very high house, and a woman of such reckless impulse and passionate prejudice that she flings her jar or pot straight from the window without thought of who is below. Broken china was to be found in plenty, but broken in some trifling domestic accident, without purpose or character. Nevertheless, he was often astonished, as he came to go into the question more deeply, by the immense variety of shapes to be found in London alone, and there was still more cause for wonder and speculation in the differences of qualities and designs. The finest specimens he would bring home and place upon his mantelpiece, where, however, their duty was more and more of an ornamental nature, since papers needing a weight to keep them down became scarcer and scarcer.

He neglected his duties, perhaps, or discharged them absent-mindedly, or his constituents when they visited him were unfavourably impressed by the appearance of his mantelpiece. At any rate he was not elected to represent them in Parliament, and his friend Charles, taking it much to heart and hurrying to condole with him, found him so little cast down by the disaster that he could only suppose that it was too serious a matter for him to realize all at once.

In truth, John had been that day to Barnes Common,

and there under a furze bush had found a very remarkable piece of iron. It was almost identical with the glass
in shape, massy and globular, but so cold and heavy, so
black and metallic, that it was evidently alien to the
earth and had its origin in one of the dead stars or was
itself the cinder of a moon. It weighed his pocket down;
it weighed the mantelpiece down; it radiated cold. And
yet the meteorite stood upon the same ledge with the
lump of glass and the star-shaped china.

As his eyes passed from one to another, the determination to possess objects that even surpassed these
tormented the young man. He devoted himself more
and more resolutely to the search. If he had not been
consumed by ambition and convinced that one day
some newly discovered rubbish heap would reward
him, the disappointments he had suffered, let alone the
fatigue and derision, would have made him give up the
pursuit. Provided with a bag and a long stick fitted with
an adaptable hook, he ransacked all deposits of earth;
raked beneath matted tangles of scrub; searched all
alleys and spaces between walls where he had learned
to expect to find objects of this kind thrown away. As
his standard became higher and his taste more severe
the disappointments were innumerable, but always
some gleam of hope, some piece of china or glass curi-
ously marked or broken, lured him on. Day after day

passed. He was no longer young. His career – that is his political career – was a thing of the past. People gave up visiting him. He was too silent to be worth asking to dinner. He never talked to anyone about his serious ambitions; their lack of understanding was apparent in their behaviour.

He leaned back in his chair now and watched Charles lift the stones on the mantelpiece a dozen times and put them down emphatically to mark what he was saying about the conduct of the Government, without once noticing their existence.

'What was the truth of it, John?' asked Charles suddenly, turning and facing him. 'What made you give it up like that all in a second?'

'I've not given it up,' John replied.

'But you've not the ghost of a chance now,' said Charles roughly.

'I don't agree with you there,' said John with conviction. Charles looked at him and was profoundly uneasy; the most extraordinary doubts possessed him; he had a queer sense that they were talking about different things. He looked round to find some relief for his horrible depression, but the disorderly appearance of the room depressed him still further. What was that stick, and the old carpet bag hanging against the wall? And then those stones? Looking at John, something fixed and distant in his expression alarmed him. He knew only too well that his mere appearance upon a platform was out of the question.

'Pretty stones,' he said as cheerfully as he could; and saying that he had an appointment to keep, he left John – for ever.

Lappin and Lapinova

They were married. The wedding march pealed out. The pigeons fluttered. Small boys in Eton jackets threw rice; a fox-terrier sauntered across the path; and Ernest Thorburn led his bride to the car through that small inquisitive crowd of complete strangers which always collects in London to enjoy other people's happiness or unhappiness. Certainly he looked handsome and she looked shy. More rice was thrown, and the car moved off.

That was on Tuesday. Now it was Saturday. Rosalind had still to get used to the fact that she was Mrs Ernest Thorburn. Perhaps she never would get used to the fact that she was Mrs Ernest Anybody, she thought, as she sat in the bow window of the hotel looking over the lake to the mountains, and waited for her husband to come down to breakfast. Ernest was a difficult name to get used to. It was not the name she would have chosen. She would have preferred Timothy, Antony, or Peter.

He did not look like Ernest either. The name suggested the Albert Memorial, mahogany sideboards, steel engravings of the Prince Consort with his family – her mother-in-law's dining-room in Porchester Terrace in short.

But here he was. Thank goodness he did not look like Ernest – no. But what did he look like? She glanced at him sideways. Well, when he was eating toast he looked like a rabbit. Not that anyone else would have seen a likeness to a creature so diminutive and timid in this spruce, muscular young man with the straight nose, the blue eyes, and the very firm mouth. But that made it all the more amusing. His nose twitched very slightly when he ate. So did her pet rabbit's. She kept watching his nose twitch; and then she had to explain, when he caught her looking at him, why she laughed.

'It's because you're like a rabbit, Ernest,' she said. 'Like a wild rabbit,' she added, looking at him. 'A hunting rabbit; a King Rabbit; a rabbit that makes laws for all the other rabbits.'

Ernest had no objection to being that kind of rabbit, and since it amused her to see him twitch his nose – he had never known that his nose twitched – he twitched it on purpose. And she laughed and laughed; and he laughed too, so that the maiden ladies and the fishing man and the Swiss waiter in his greasy black jacket all guessed right; they were very happy. But how long does such happiness last? they asked themselves; and each answered according to his own circumstances.

At lunch time, seated on a clump of heather beside the lake, 'Lettuce, rabbit?' said Rosalind, holding out the lettuce that had been provided to eat with the hard-boiled eggs. 'Come and take it out of my hand,' she added, and he stretched out and nibbled the lettuce and twitched his nose.

'Good rabbit, nice rabbit,' she said, patting him, as she used to pat her tame rabbit at home. But that was absurd. He was not a tame rabbit, whatever he was. She turned it into French. 'Lapin,' she called him. But whatever he was, he was not a French rabbit. He was simply and solely English – born in Porchester Terrace, educated at Rugby; now a clerk in His Majesty's Civil Service. So she tried 'Bunny' next; but that was worse. 'Bunny' was someone plump and soft and comic; he was thin and hard and serious. Still, his nose twitched. 'Lappin,' she exclaimed suddenly; and gave a little cry as if she had found the very word she looked for.

'Lappin, Lappin, King Lappin,' she repeated. It seemed to suit him exactly; he was not Ernest, he was King Lappin. Why? She did not know.

When there was nothing new to talk about on their long solitary walks – and it rained, as everyone had warned them that it would rain; or when they were sitting over the fire in the evening, for it was cold, and the maiden ladies had gone and the fishing man, and the waiter only came if you rang the bell for him, she let her fancy play with the story of the Lappin tribe. Under her hands – she was sewing, he was reading – they became very real, very vivid, very amusing. Ernest put down the paper and helped her. There were the black rabbits and the red; there were the enemy rabbits and the friendly. There were the wood in which they lived and the outlying prairies and the swamp. Above all there was King Lappin, who, far from having only the one trick – that he twitched his nose – became, as the days passed, an animal of the greatest character. Rosalind was always finding new qualities in him. But above all he was a great hunter.

'And what,' said Rosalind, on the last day of the honeymoon, 'did the King do to-day?'

In fact they had been climbing all day; and she had worn a blister on her heel; but she did not mean that.

'To-day,' said Ernest twitching his nose as he bit the end off his cigar, 'he chased a hare.' He paused; struck a match, and twitched again.

'A woman hare,' he added.

'A white hare!' Rosalind exclaimed, as if she had been

expecting this. 'Rather a small hare; silver grey; with big bright eyes?'

'Yes,' said Ernest, looking at her as she had looked at him, 'a smallish animal; with eyes popping out of her head, and two little front paws dangling.' It was exactly how she sat, with her sewing dangling in her hands; and her eyes, that were so big and bright, were certainly a little prominent.

'Ah, Lapinova,' Rosalind murmured.

'Is that what she's called,' said Ernest, 'the real Rosalind?' He looked at her. He felt very much in love with her.

'Yes; that's what she's called,' said Rosalind: 'Lapinova.' And before they went to bed that night it was all settled. He was King Lappin; she was Queen Lapinova. They were the very opposite of each other; he was bold and determined; she wary and undependable. He ruled over the busy world of rabbits; her world was a desolate, mysterious place, which she ranged mostly by moonlight. All the same, their territories touched; they were King and Queen of the land of rabbits and hares.

Thus when they came back from their honeymoon they possessed a private world, inhabited, save for the one white hare, entirely by rabbits. No one guessed that

there was such a place, and that of course made it all
the more amusing. It made them feel, more even than
most young married couples, in league together against
the rest of the world. Often they looked slyly at each
other when people talked about rabbits and woods and
traps and shooting. Or they winked furtively across the
table when Aunt Mary said that she could never bear to
see a hare in a dish – it looked so like a baby; or when
John, Ernest's sporting brother, told them what price
rabbits were fetching that autumn in Wiltshire, skins
and all. Sometimes when they wanted a gamekeeper, or
a poacher or a Lord of the Manor, they amused themselves by distributing the parts among their friends.
Ernest's mother, Mrs Reginald Thorburn, for example,
fitted the part of the Squire to perfection. But it was all
secret – that was the point of it; nobody save themselves
knew that such a world existed.

Without that world, how, Rosalind wondered, could
she ever have endured the golden-wedding party when all
the Thorburns assembled at Porchester Terrace to cele-
brate the fiftieth anniversary of that union which had
been so blessed – had it not produced Ernest Thorburn? –
and so fruitful – had it not produced nine other sons
and daughters into the bargain, many themselves married and also fruitful? She dreaded that party. But it was
inevitable. As she walked upstairs she felt bitterly that

she was an only child and an orphan at that; a mere drop among all those Thorburns assembled in the great drawing-room with the shiny satin wallpaper and the lustrous family portraits. The living Thorburns much resembled the painted; save that instead of painted lips they had real lips; out of which came jokes; jokes about schoolrooms, and how they had pulled the chair from under the governess; jokes about frogs and how they had put them between the virgin sheets of maiden ladies. As for herself, she had never even made an apple-pie bed. Holding her present in her hand, she advanced towards her mother-in-law, sumptuous in yellow satin; and towards her father-in-law, decorated with a rich yellow carnation. All round them on tables and chairs there were golden tributes, some nestling in cotton wool; others branching resplendent – candlesticks; cigar boxes; chains; each stamped with the goldsmith's proof that it was solid gold, hallmarked, authentic. But her present was only a little pinchbeck box pierced with holes; an old sand caster, an eighteenth-century relic, once used to sprinkle sand over wet ink. Rather a senseless present, she felt, in an age of blotting-paper; and as she proffered it, she saw in front of her the stubby black handwriting in which her mother-in-law, when they were engaged, had expressed the hope that 'My son will make you happy.' No, she was not happy. Not at all happy. She looked at Ernest, straight as a ramrod with a nose like all the noses in the family portraits, a nose that never twitched at all.

Then they went down to dinner. She was half hidden by the great chrysanthemums that curled their red and gold petals into large tight balls. Everything was gold. A gold-edged card with gold initials intertwined recited the list of all the dishes that would be set one after another before them. She dipped her spoon in a plate of clear golden soup. The raw white fog outside had been turned by the lamps into a golden mesh that blurred the edges of the plates and gave the pineapples a rough golden skin. Only she herself in her white wedding dress peering ahead of her with her prominent eyes seemed insoluble as an icicle.

As the dinner wore on, however, the room grew steamy with heat. Beads of perspiration stood out on the men's foreheads. She felt that her icicle was being turned to water. She was being melted; dispersed; dissolved into nothingness; and would soon faint. Then through the surge in her head and the din in her ears she heard a woman's voice exclaim, 'But of course they breed so!'

The Thorburns – yes; they breed so, she echoed; looking at all the round red faces that seemed doubled in the giddiness that overcame her; and magnified in the gold mist that enhaloed them. 'They breed so.' Then John bawled:

'Little devils! Shoot 'em! Jump on 'em with big boots! That's the only way to deal with 'em . . . rabbits!'

At that word, that magic word, she revived. Peeping between the chrysanthemums she saw Ernest's nose twitch. It rippled, it ran, with successive twitches. And at that a mysterious catastrophe befell the Thorburns. The golden table became a moor with the gorse in full bloom; the din of voices turned to one peal of lark's laughter ringing down from the sky. It was a blue sky – clouds passed slowly. And they had all been changed – the Thorburns. She looked at her father-in-law, a furtive little man with dyed moustaches. His foible was collecting things – seals, enamel boxes, trifles from eighteenth-century dressing-tables which he hid from his wife in the drawers of his desk. Now she saw him as he was – a poacher, stealing off with his coat bulging with pheasants and partridges to drop them stealthily into a three-legged pot in his smoky little cottage. That was her real father-in-law – a poacher. And Celia, the unmarried daughter, who always nosed out other people's secrets, the little things they wished to hide – she was a white ferret with pink eyes, and a nose clotted with earth from her horrid underground nosings and pokings. Slung round men's shoulders, in a net, and thrust down a hole – it was a pitiable life, Celia's; it was none of her fault. So she saw Celia. And then she looked at her mother-in-law – whom they dubbed The Squire. Flushed, coarse, a bully – she was all that, as she stood returning thanks, but now that Rosalind – that is Lapinova – saw her, she saw behind her the decayed family mansion, the plaster peeling off the walls, and heard her, with a sob in her voice, giving thanks to her children (who hated her) for a world that had ceased to exist. There was a sudden silence. They all stood with their glasses raised; they all drank; then it was over.

'Oh, King Lappin!' she cried as they went home together in the fog. 'If your nose hadn't twitched just at that moment, I should have been trapped!'

'But you're safe,' said King Lappin, pressing her paw.

'Quite safe,' she answered, pressing his too.

And they drove back through the Park, King and Queen of the marsh, of the mist, of the gorse-scented moor.

Thus time passed; one year; two years of time. And on a winter's night, which happened by a coincidence to be the **anniversary** of the golden-wedding party – but Mrs Reginald Thorburn was dead; the house was to let; and there was only a caretaker in residence – Ernest came home from the office. They had a nice little home; half a house above a saddler's shop in South Kensington, not far from the Tube station. It was cold, with fog in the air, and Rosalind was sitting over the fire, sewing.

'What d'you think happened to me to-day?' she began as soon as he had settled himself down with his legs stretched to the blaze. 'I was crossing the stream when –'

'What stream?' Ernest interrupted her.

'The stream at the bottom, where our wood meets the black wood,' she explained.

Ernest looked completely blank for a moment.

'What the deuce are you talking about?' he asked.

'My dear Ernest!' she cried in dismay. 'King Lappin,' she added, dangling her little front paws in the firelight. But his nose did not twitch. Her hands – they turned to hands – clutched the stuff she was holding; her eyes popped half out of her head. It took him five minutes at least to change from Ernest Thorburn to King Lappin; and while she waited she felt a load on the back of her neck, as if somebody were about to wring it. At last he changed to King Lappin; his nose twitched; and they spent the evening roaming the woods much as usual.

But she slept badly. In the middle of the night she woke, feeling as if something strange had happened to her. She was stiff and cold. At last she turned on the light and looked at Ernest lying beside her. He was sound asleep. He snored. But even though he snored, his nose remained perfectly still. It looked as if it had never twitched at all. Was it possible that he was really Ernest; and that she was really married to Ernest? A vision of her mother-in-law's dining-room came before her; and there they sat, she and Ernest, grown old, under the engravings, in front of the sideboard . . . It was their golden-wedding day. She could not bear it.

'Lappin, King Lappin!' she whispered, and for a moment his nose seemed to twitch of its own accord. But he still slept. 'Wake up, Lappin, wake up!' she cried.

Ernest woke; and, seeing her sitting bolt upright beside him, he asked:

'What's the matter?'

'I thought my rabbit was dead!' she whimpered. Ernest was angry.

'Don't talk such rubbish, Rosalind,' he said. 'Lie down and go to sleep.'

He turned over. In another moment he was sound asleep and snoring.

But she could not sleep. She lay curled up on her side

of the bed, like a hare in its form. She had turned out the light, but the street-lamp lit the ceiling faintly, and the trees outside made a lacy network over it as if there were a shadowy grove on the ceiling in which she wandered, turning, twisting, in and out, round and round, hunting, being hunted, hearing the bay of hounds, and horns blowing . . . until the maid drew the blinds and brought their early tea.

Next day she could settle to nothing. She seemed to have lost something. She felt as if her body had shrunk; it had grown small, and black and hard. Her joints seemed stiff too, and when she looked in the glass, which she did several times as she wandered about the flat, her eyes seemed to burst out of her head, like currants in a bun. The rooms also seemed to have shrunk. Large pieces of furniture jutted out at odd angles and she found herself knocking against them. At last she put on her hat and went out. She walked along the Cromwell Road; and every room she passed and peered into seemed to be a dining-room where people sat eating under steel engravings, with thick yellow lace curtains, and mahogany sideboards. At last she reached the Natural History Museum; she used to like it when she was a child. But the first thing she saw when she went in was a stuffed hare standing on sham snow with pink glass eyes. Somehow it made her shiver all over. Perhaps it would be better when dusk fell. She went home and sat over the fire, without a light, and tried to imagine that she was out alone on a moor: and there was a stream rushing; and beyond the stream a dark wood. But she could get no farther than the stream. At last she squatted down on the bank on the wet grass, and sat crouched in her chair, with her hands dangling empty, and her eyes glazed, like glass eyes, in the fire-light. Then there was the crack of a gun . . . She started as if she had been shot. It was only Ernest turning his key in the door. She waited, trembling. He came in and switched on the light. There he stood tall, handsome, rubbing his hands that were red with cold.

'Sitting in the dark?' he said.

'Oh, Ernest, Ernest!' she cried starting up in her chair.

'Well, what's up now?' he asked briskly, warming his hands at the fire.

'It's Lapinova . . .' she faltered, glancing wildly at him out of her great startled eyes. 'She's gone, Ernest. I've lost her!'

Ernest frowned. He pressed his lips tight together. 'Oh, that's what's up, is it?' he said, smiling rather grimly at his wife. For ten seconds he stood there, silent; and she waited, feeling hands tightening at the back of her neck.

'Yes,' he said at length. 'Poor Lapinova . . .' He straightened his tie at the looking-glass.

'Caught in a trap,' he said. 'Killed,' and sat down and read the newspaper.

So that was the end of that marriage.

Ryūnosuke Akutagawa *Hell Screen*

Kingsley Amis *Dear Illusion*

Donald Barthelme *Some of Us Had Been Threatening Our Friend Colby*

Samuel Beckett *The Expelled*

Saul Bellow *Him With His Foot in His Mouth*

Jorge Luis Borges *The Widow Ching – Pirate*

Paul Bowles *The Delicate Prey*

Italo Calvino *The Queen's Necklace*

Albert Camus *The Adulterous Woman*

Truman Capote *Children on Their Birthdays*

Angela Carter *Bluebeard*

Raymond Chandler *Killer in the Rain*

Eileen Chang *Red Rose, White Rose*

G. K. Chesterton *The Strange Crime of John Boulnois*

Joseph Conrad *Youth*

Robert Coover *Romance of the Thin Man and the Fat Lady*

Isak Dinesen [Karen Blixen] *Babette's Feast*

Margaret Drabble *The Gifts of War*

Hans Fallada *Short Treatise on the Joys of Morphinism*

F. Scott Fitzgerald *Babylon Revisited*

Ian Fleming *The Living Daylights*

E. M. Forster *The Machine Stops*

Shirley Jackson *The Tooth*

Henry James *The Beast in the Jungle*

M. R. JAMES *Canon Alberic's Scrap-Book*

JAMES JOYCE *Two Gallants*

FRANZ KAFKA *In the Penal Colony*

RUDYARD KIPLING *'They'*

D. H. LAWRENCE *Odour of Chrysanthemums*

PRIMO LEVI *The Magic Paint*

H. P. LOVECRAFT *The Colour Out of Space*

MALCOLM LOWRY *Lunar Caustic*

CARSON MCCULLERS *Wunderkind*

KATHERINE MANSFIELD *Bliss*

ROBERT MUSIL *Flypaper*

VLADIMIR NABOKOV *Terra Incognita*

R. K. NARAYAN *A Breath of Lucifer*

FRANK O'CONNOR *The Cornet-Player Who Betrayed Ireland*

DOROTHY PARKER *The Sexes*

LUDMILLA PETRUSHEVSKAYA *Through the Wall*

JEAN RHYS *La Grosse Fifi*

SAKI *Filboid Studge, the Story of a Mouse That Helped*

ISAAC BASHEVIS SINGER *The Last Demon*

WILLIAM TREVOR *The Mark-2 Wife*

JOHN UPDIKE *Rich in Russia*

H. G. WELLS *The Door in the Wall*

EUDORA WELTY *Moon Lake*

P. G. WODEHOUSE *The Crime Wave at Blandings*

VIRGINIA WOOLF *The Lady in the Looking-Glass*

STEFAN ZWEIG *Chess*

a little history

Penguin Modern Classics were launched in 1961, and have been shaping the reading habits of generations ever since.

The list began with distinctive grey spines and evocative pictorial covers – a look that, after various incarnations, continues to influence their current design – and with books that are still considered landmark classics today.

Penguin Modern Classics have caused scandal and political change, inspired great films and broken down barriers, whether social, sexual or the boundaries of language itself. They remain the most provocative, groundbreaking, exciting and revolutionary works of the last 100 years (or so).

In 2011, on the fiftieth anniversary of the Modern Classics, we're publishing fifty Mini Modern Classics: the very best short fiction by writers ranging from Beckett to Conrad, Nabokov to Saki, Updike to Wodehouse. Though they don't take long to read, they'll stay with you long after you turn the final page.

MODERN CLASSICS
www.penguinclassics.com